Cumbria County Co[unt]
Education Authority
Leven Valley C.E. S[chool]
Backbarrow, Ulvers[ton]

D0349615

Andrew's Bath

David McPhail

Blackie

Copyright © 1984 David McPhail
First published 1984 by Little, Brown & Company, USA,
in association with Atlantic Monthly Press
This edition published 1987 by Blackie and Son Ltd

All rights reserved. No part of this publication may be reproduced,
stored in a retrieval system, or transmitted in any form
or by any means, electronic, mechanical, photocopying, recording
or otherwise without the written permission of the Publishers.

British Library Cataloguing in Publication Data
McPhail, David, *1940–*
Andrew's bath.
I. Title
813′ .54 [J]   PZ7

ISBN 0–216–92090–6

Blackie and Son Limited
7 Leicester Place
London WC2H 7BP

Filmset by Deltatype,
Ellesmere Port

For my pal Roli

Andrew was forever having trouble with his bath.

Either it was too hot,

or too cold,

too shallow,

or too deep.

His mother scrubbed him too hard,

or his father used too much shampoo.
Giving Andrew a bath wasn't easy.

'I think Andrew is big enough to give himself a bath,'
said Andrew's mother one day.
'I think you're right,' said Andrew's father.

That night, Andrew went upstairs
to give himself his very own bath.

First he filled the tub.
The water was not too hot, not too cold,
not too shallow, and not too deep.

He collected all his favourite toys
and books.

He took off all his clothes,

and climbed into the bath.

Downstairs, Andrew's mother thought she
could hear water splashing on the floor.
'What's going on up there?' she asked.

'There's a frog in the bath,' answered Andrew.
'And it's splashing water all over the floor!'
'Well, tell it to stop,' said Andrew's mother.

A little later, Andrew's father called
to Andrew. 'Are you washing?'

'I can't!' said Andrew. 'There's a hippo
in the bath and it's sitting on the soap!'

'Tell the hippo to get up,' said Andrew's father.
'And scrub behind your ears with your flannel!'

'I can't!' said Andrew. 'An alligator bit it
and he won't let go!'

'Then take it away from him!' said Andrew's father.

'I did!' said Andrew. 'But now it's all
ripped and full of tooth holes!'

'Never mind,' said Andrew's mother, looking
at Andrew's father. 'Just wash your hair!'

'I can't' said Andrew.
'The elephant drank all the shampoo!'

'That's enough!' Andrew's father shouted.
'Let the water out of the bath this instant.'

'I'm trying,' said Andrew. 'But there's
a thirsty lion in here and he won't let me.'

'Andrew,' called his mother.
'Get out of the bath and dry off right now!'

'I am! I am!' cried Andrew.

Andrew hurried downstairs to say good-night.
'Can the animals sleep with me tonight?' he asked.
Andrew's mother and father just looked at each
other. 'Only if they are quiet,' they said.

'Oh, they will be!' cried Andrew.
And he hurried off to bed.